# Chu's Day

Neil Gaiman

Illustrated By
Adam Rex

**HARPER**
*An Imprint of HarperCollinsPublishers*

For Zixuan Li, a swan and a plum.
–N.G.

For Steve.
–A.R.

Library of Congress Cataloging-in-Publication Data is available.
ISBN 978-0-06-201781-9

Typography by Alison Carmichael 13 14 15 16 17 LP 10 9 8 7 6 5 4 3 2 ❖ First Edition

When Chu sneezed,

bad things happened.

In the morning, Chu went with his mother to the library.

There was old-book-dust
in the air.

"Are you going to sneeze?"
said his mother.

aah-

aaah-

Aaaah-

No, said Chu.

At lunchtime, Chu went with
his father to the diner.

There was a lot of pepper
in the air....

"Are you going to sneeze?" asked his father.

AAH-

AAAAH-

AAAAAH-

No, said Chu.

Later that day,
Chu and his parents went to
the circus!

I will tell you something,
said Chu.

Guess what? said Chu.
But nobody listened.
They were watching the circus.

I think I am going to sneeze, said Chu.

AAaachooc

OOOOOO!

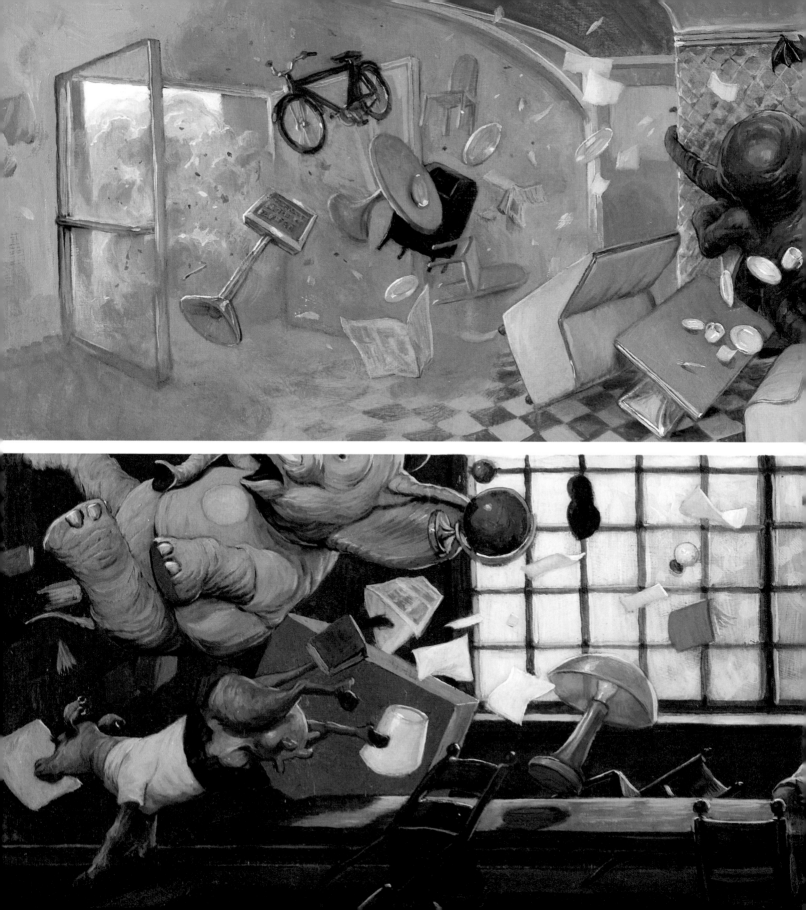

Oops, said Chu.

After the circus, Chu went
to bed.

Yup, said Chu.
That was a sneeze all right.

Goodnight.